Contents

People in the story

Will Traynor

Lou Clark

Lissa

Patrick

Mrs Traynor

Nathan

Treena

Rupert

New words

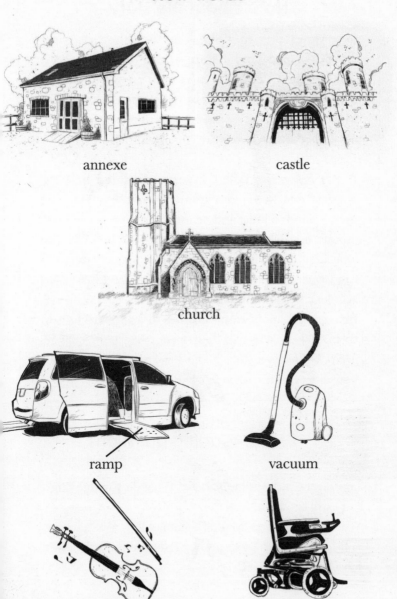

annexe

castle

church

ramp

vacuum

violin

wheelchair

5

Note about the story

Jojo Moyes lives in Essex, England. She first wrote for newspapers and began writing books in 2002. The idea for *Me Before You* came from a news story about a **disabled*** sportsman who wanted to end his life. Moyes has written two more novels about the people in *Me Before You*: the novels are *Still Me* and *After You*.

In *Me Before You*, Will Traynor is **disabled** in a car accident and becomes a **quadriplegic**. Will can still use his hands a little, and he uses them to move himself around in a **wheelchair**. His family pay Lou Clark to look after him. Will and Lou's families are very different from each other. Will's family are rich, and before his accident he had an exciting life. Lou's family do not have enough money, and Lou has to work hard to help them. When Will and Lou meet, they both change. *Me Before You* is a story about love, but it is also about how difficult life can be for disabled people.

Before-reading questions

1 Look at the pictures in the book. What do you think the story will be about?
2 Will and Lou come from different families. Will's is rich, and Lou's is poor. What problems do you think they will have when they meet?

*Definitions of words in **bold** can be found in the glossary on pages 78–80.

CHAPTER ONE

A rainy morning

February 2007

When Will came out of the bathroom, Lissa was sitting up in his bed and looking through a travel **magazine**. Her beautiful blonde hair fell over her **shoulders**.

"Do we really have to walk up mountains?" she said. "It will be our first holiday together. How about a beach in Bali? We can lie on the sand and have long, **relaxing** evenings."

"I don't like relaxing holidays," Will replied, putting on a **suit**. "I need to be busy."

"Like throwing yourself out of aeroplanes, or **bungee jumping**?" Lissa asked and smiled.

"You should try it," he replied. "Right, I must go to the office. There's food in the fridge for breakfast."

He sat on the side of the bed, and she put her arms around his neck. "I'll have breakfast when I get home," she said. "Are we going away this weekend?"

"I'm not sure," he replied, kissing her. Then he stood up and turned on his mobile phone, which immediately showed that he had lots of messages. "I may have to go to New York. Shall we go out for dinner on Thursday? You can choose the restaurant."

"I will only come if you turn off that thing," she said, looking at his phone.

He smiled. "OK, I promise to turn it off." Then he put on his jacket and left his flat.

When Will got to the street, it was raining hard, and he decided to get a taxi. While he was waiting for one to arrive, he began checking his messages. He listened to the first one and immediately made a call.

"You have to call New York, Rupert," he said. "Something's wrong with the papers."

A taxi came along the other side of the road. Will looked from left to right and then began to run across the road. The rain was running down his neck. Suddenly, he heard an engine and then the sound of wheels stopping quickly. He turned, and for a second he saw the huge car coming fast towards him. Then his hand opened and the phone fell on to the road.

And then there was nothing.

CHAPTER TWO
A bad day

February 2009

The day started like other days. I enjoyed my job at the Buttered Bun Café in Stortford. It was not a **posh** place. The tables were cheap and red, and most of the pictures on the wall were of Stortford Castle, which was up on the hill behind the café. But I liked making the tea in the mornings with the smell of warm bread and the sound of quiet conversations around me. I liked the customers the most. I liked the old lady who came every day and had one egg and chips. I liked the workmen who came for their lunch. I liked the tourists who stopped on their walk back from the castle and the loud schoolchildren who came in after school.

Frank owned the café. He came from Australia. He was quiet, but I talked a lot, and he liked that. "You make the place noisy and happy," he said. "And they like your crazy clothes." Working in the Buttered Bun was like working in a pub but without the problem of **drunk** people.

But that afternoon, when lunch was finished and we were quiet, something different happened. Frank walked to the door and turned round the "Closed" sign.

"Sorry, Louisa," he said, "but I'm going back to Australia. My dad isn't well, and the castle is going to open its own café. Tourists will use the new café instead of mine."

I sat with my mouth open. I was shocked. "I'm sorry about your Dad," I said slowly. Then Frank put something in my hand. "Here's three months' money," he said, "and I'll give you a good **reference**, of course. We close tomorrow."

"He's only given you three months' money?" shouted Dad, while my mother put a cup of tea in my hands. "Well, that's good of him. When did you start working there – six years ago?"

I knew why Dad was worried. My family really needed the money that the café paid me. My sister, Treena, who I shared a bedroom with, was paid very little from her job at the flower shop. And she was going to start college soon, so that meant even less money was going to come into the house. Mum could not work because she had to look after Grandad, who also lived with us. Grandad was old and often got ill. Dad worked in a factory that made **furniture**, and he knew that the business was not doing well and that he might be made **redundant**. I often heard my parents talking quietly about money.

"She'll have to go to the **job centre** tomorrow," Mum said. "She's clever. You're clever, aren't you, Lou? Maybe she can train to do office work."

I sat quietly as my parents talked about the different jobs that I could do. For the first time, I felt like crying.

I went to find my boyfriend, Patrick, at the running club. He always trained there in the evenings from Mondays to Thursdays. I found him running round the track. "Run with me," he said.

I began running next to him. "I got bored at home," I said. "Mum's busy, and Dad's sleeping because he's working during the nights this week. Shall we go to the cinema?"

"Sorry, but I've got to train. You need to get another job as soon as possible," he said.

"I only left the café twenty-four hours ago," I replied, **breathing** hard. "Can't I relax for one day?"

Patrick had a **personal training** business, with an office and two cars. He was making a lot of money, and he liked telling me about it.

He was running faster than me, and he began to move ahead of me.

"You need to get a better job," he shouted over his shoulder. "You can change your life now, Lou. You can go to college, or train to do something different. You can't just sit around at home. Put on a suit, and go to the job centre. Or I'll train you to work with me."

The next day, I went to the job centre. There was a forty-five-minute **interview** with a man called Syed. I got a week of work at a chicken factory. Then I worked for two weeks at a burger restaurant, but they told me what to say. Every time a customer came in, I had to ask questions like, "How are you today?" and, "Would you like large fries with that?" and not say other things. But I spoke to the customers like a normal person and **joked** with them, so the restaurant told me to leave. I went back to the job centre for my third interview.

Syed sat opposite me. "There aren't many jobs left. You wrote that you like working with people and talking to them. So how do you feel about becoming a **care assistant**?" he said, looking at his computer.

"You won't have to look after lots of old people," he added, quickly. "You'll work for a family. You will be helping in someone's house. They only live two miles from your home. It says, 'Care and **company** for a **disabled** man'. Can you drive?"

"Yes," I said, "but do I have to . . . you know . . . wash him and help him go to the toilet?"

"No," Syed replied. "He's a **quadriplegic**, and he's got a nurse. He needs someone there in the day to **feed** him, look after him and talk to him. He needs help when he wants to go out and with anything he can't do for himself. The money is good. Will you go for the interview?"

It was a question – but we both knew the answer.

CHAPTER THREE
The interview

"You can't wear your usual crazy clothes – you must wear a suit to the interview," Mum said, looking down at my green skirt and red boots. "You can borrow mine." The suit looked nice, but the skirt was a bit small. "And please don't wear purple **tights** with it, or one of your strange hats. Try to look like a normal person."

I took the bus to Granta House, which was on the other side of Stortford Castle to our house. It was huge and posh, like a house you saw in magazines. When I walked up to it, the door suddenly opened, and a woman came out. She was in her forties or fifties, and she was still beautiful. She was wearing an expensive-looking suit.

"Are you Miss Clark?" she said in a posh voice.

"Yes. I'm Louisa," I said.

"Please come in. My name is Camilla Traynor." She sounded tired.

I followed her to a huge room with high windows and lots of paintings.

"Please sit down," she said.

I sat down and waited while she looked through her papers, and then I heard it – the sound of my skirt **tearing**. I felt my face turn red.

"So, Miss Clark. Do you have any experience of working with quadriplegics?" Mrs Traynor asked.

"No," I replied, and I tried to pull my suit jacket down over the **tear**.

"Do you know what a quadriplegic is?"

"Erm . . ." I said, not feeling sure. "Is it when you're in a **wheelchair**?"

"Well, yes, you can say that," Mrs Traynor replied without smiling. "My son cannot use his legs, and he can only move his hands a little. It's enough to move his wheelchair around the annexe, but not much more. Is that a problem for you?"

"It's not as much a problem for me as it is a problem for him," I joked and smiled, but she did not smile back.

The tear was getting bigger. I was frightened to stand up because I knew that she would see it.

"I have a reference from your last job," she said. "It says you are a 'warm, kind and funny person'."

"I paid him to write that," I joked.

Still she did not smile. "And what do you want to do with your life?" she asked.

"I . . . I . . . don't know," I replied, stupidly. "I just want to work again."

Mrs Traynor put down her pen. "Miss Clark, this job is only for six months," she said. "That's why the money is . . . well, good. We want the right person. My son, Will, was in a road accident two years ago. He has to be looked after day and night. He has a nurse, and the new person will need to be here from eight to five to help Will with food and drink – and to talk to him. We want somebody who is happy and friendly." Mrs Traynor stood up, and I guessed that was the end of the interview.

"I see," I said, and I began to stand up, too. I tried to pull my bag over the tear, but I knew that she could see it.

"So would you like the job?" she asked, walking towards the door. "We need you to start as soon as possible."

For a moment I couldn't speak.

"You will learn that Will is not an easy person to be with," she continued. "So will we see you tomorrow?"

"Won't I meet him today?" I asked.

"He's not having a good day today. It's better if you start tomorrow," she replied. She was already by the door, waiting for me.

"Yes," I said. "Thank you. I'll see you at eight o'clock tomorrow morning."

"This is the annexe," Mrs Traynor said the next morning.

"It's good for Will because there are no stairs. That's Will's room, and there is another bedroom for Nathan, his nurse, when he needs to stay here. He stayed here a lot immediately after the accident."

She walked quickly through the hall, opening door after door. "The keys to his car are there," she said. "You can drive it. It has a special ramp, and Nathan will show you how it works. This is the kitchen. You can make yourself tea and coffee here," she said, walking into a large, clean kitchen with a white floor. Then she turned. "It's very important that Will is never alone for more than fifteen minutes. If you have to go out, please call me or my husband. If you're ill or can't work for a day, please let us know as soon as possible."

"I won't go anywhere," I replied.

"When Will is doing something, please do some cleaning if the annexe needs it," she said, coming to a door. "Wash the bed **sheets**, **vacuum** the floors. He may want to be alone sometimes, but please stay near him. I hope you will be friends. Are you ready to meet him?" And without waiting for my answer, she knocked on the door. "Miss Clark is here, Will. Can we come in?" she called.

There was no answer. She pushed open the door to the living room, which was very large and had a fire burning in one corner. One wall was glass, and you could see trees and hills through it.

In the middle of the room, a man was sitting in a black

wheelchair. Another man was kneeling on the floor in front of him, putting on the shoes of the man in the wheelchair.

The man in the wheelchair had long, untidy hair. When I entered the room, he suddenly screamed loudly again and again, and he started moving his head up and down.

"Will! Please!" shouted his mother. "Please don't!"

"Oh God, I can't do this," I thought. Then the man stopped screaming and looked at me.

"I . . . I'm Lou," I said. "It's short for Louisa."

He smiled. "Good morning, Miss Clark," he said.

The other man stood up. He was short, but his body looked strong. "You're a bad man, Will," he said and smiled. "Very bad." Then he held out his hand. "I'm Nathan,

Will's nurse. Will likes to act like he's crazy. It frightens his care assistants. But he's not really bad."

Mrs Traynor started to move back through the door. "I'll leave you all now," she said. "Please call me if you need help, Louisa."

She disappeared, and we listened to the sound of her feet walking across the hall outside. "Miss Clark, can I tell you about what Will needs?" said Nathan, after a moment.

"Of course."

I followed him into the kitchen. "OK, it's quite simple," he explained. "Everything you need to know is here. He has these two **pills** every day. One in the morning, one at night. Then he needs these pills for his stomach . . ." Nathan continued to show me lots of pills for Will's many different problems.

"It's a lot to remember," I said when he finished.

"It's all written here," he replied, and he gave me some papers. "I will **lift** him when he needs it and change his bag when he needs the toilet. He . . . he's not always an easy person to be with, but I like him."

I followed him back to the living room. Will was sitting at the window with his back to us. "I've finished work for the morning," said Nathan. "Do you need anything else, Will?"

"No, thank you, Nathan," replied Will, without turning round.

"I'll be back at lunchtime," Nathan said, putting on his jacket, smiling at me. "Have fun." Then he was gone.

CHAPTER FOUR
Lou meets Will

I stood in the middle of the room. Will continued to look out of the window.

"Would you like me to make you a cup of tea?" I said at last.

"Ah, the girl who makes tea," he replied. "No. No thank you, Miss Clark."

"Well, can I get you anything?"

He turned around to look at me through his untidy hair. He had a lot of hair on his **cheeks**, and he needed a **shave**. Then he turned away without speaking.

"I'll see if there's any washing," I said.

I found some dirty bed sheets and put them in the washing machine. Then I vacuumed around the two bedrooms.

One bedroom was almost empty, like a hotel room, but Will's room had lots of photographs in it. There was a picture of him bungee jumping, and another of him climbing a mountain. Then I saw one with his arm round a girl who wore sunglasses and had long blonde hair. I knelt down to look at it.

"France. Two and a half years ago," said a voice.

I got up quickly to see Will sitting outside the bedroom door and looking at me.

"I'm sorry. I was just . . ."

"You were just looking at my photographs," he said.

"You were thinking, 'How could he go from that wonderful life to being disabled?'"

"No." But I felt my face go red.

"There are more photographs in the cupboard if you want to see them," he said, and then he turned the wheelchair to the right and disappeared.

———

The morning passed very slowly. I tried to find jobs to do and stayed away from the living room. At 11 a.m., I took Will some water and gave him his pills. He **swallowed** the pills and then said he wanted to be alone.

The kitchen was already clean, but I cleaned it again. Nathan came at 12.30 p.m., and I went out for half an hour. I walked around the streets and breathed the cold winter air. Then I rang my sister.

"Treena, he hates me," I said.

"I can't believe that you're already thinking about leaving," replied Treena. "He's unhappy. He's in a wheelchair. Just talk to him, Lou. You can't leave. We need the money."

She was right. But then she was *always* right. Sometimes I hated my sister!

———

"So, would you like to go somewhere?" I said after Nathan left. "I could drive you."

Will turned his face towards me. "Where?" he asked.

"I don't know," I replied.

"What will we see?" he asked. "Some trees? Some sky?

Do you think that going outside will be good for me?"

"I don't know . . . I . . ."

"Miss Clark, my life will not get better because you drive me somewhere," he said, and he turned the wheelchair away from me.

I was silent for a moment. Then I said, "We have to spend a lot of time together. Could you tell me more about yourself? What do you want to do? What do you like? Then I could help you more."

Finally, the wheelchair turned round again. "Here's what I know about you, Miss Clark," he said, slowly. "You talk a lot. Can we agree something? Can you *not* talk a lot near me?"

I swallowed and felt my face go red. "Fine," I said, when I could speak again. "I'll be in the kitchen. If you want anything, please call me."

———

Two weeks passed, and we slowly started a **routine**. I always arrived at Granta House at 8 a.m. Then, after Nathan finished helping Will to put on his clothes, I turned on the television or radio for him and gave him his pills. Then I washed and cleaned around the annexe, and I went into the living room every fifteen minutes to check on him. Usually, he was sitting in his chair and looking out at the garden. Later, I gave him water and gave him food with a spoon. He hated me doing this and never looked at me. In the afternoon, I usually put on a film for him, but he never wanted me to watch it with him. He was horrible to me, and I often felt stupid. I began to hate the job, but I knew that my family needed the money, so I stayed.

Sometimes, Mrs Traynor came in and said, "Everything all right?" I always said, "Yes." Then she always looked at Will. But he never looked at her and often did not answer her questions.

Will's father, who was a large, kind man, usually came home when I was leaving. His last job was in a bank in the City of London, but now he looked after Stortford Castle. He finished work every day at 5 p.m. and came to the annexe to watch some television with Will.

———————

One morning, a man and woman came to see Will. The woman had long legs and blonde hair, and she was posh and beautiful. Her clothes and bag looked very expensive. Then I looked at her more closely and saw that she was the woman in the photograph in Will's bedroom.

She kissed Will on the cheek. "You look well," she said. "You really do."

"New chair?" asked the man, and he hit the back of Will's wheelchair.

They asked him a few more questions, and then there was a difficult **silence**. I went to put some more wood on the fire. Finally, Will said, "So why have you come to see me? It's been eight months . . ."

"Oh, I know, I'm sorry," said the woman. "I've been very busy with my new job at Sasha's dress shop in Chelsea. I called a few times. Didn't your mother tell you?"

"And I've been very busy at the office," said the man.

Everyone went silent again for a minute. Then the woman said, "Actually, Rupert and I came because we have some news. We're getting married."

I stood up slowly from the fire and looked at Will. His face did not move.

"I know it's a shock," the woman continued. "We, it . . . it only started a long time after . . ."

"I'm very happy for you," Will said, suddenly, but he did not smile.

"Will, I know what you're thinking," the woman said, quickly, "but we really didn't plan this. Rupert helped me so much after . . ."

"That was *good* of him," Will replied, angrily.

Rupert suddenly moved forward. "Look, Will, we're only telling you because we care about you. Life goes on.

It's been two years now. You must want Lissa to have a good life."

Will did not answer.

"Come on, Lissa," Rupert said. "We should leave."

The two people started to move slowly towards the door.

When they were gone, I went into the kitchen and made a cup of tea that I did not want. I waited for a few minutes and then went back to the living room, but Will was not there. Then I heard the sound of breaking glass. I turned and ran into his bedroom. He was turning his wheelchair and moving it side to side, and he was knocking the pictures on to the floor with his knees.

He heard me enter, and his chair turned on the bits of glass. His eyes met mine in a long, angry silence.

"I hope your wheels are OK," I said, finally. "Because there isn't a garage near here."

His eyes became bigger. I thought that he was going to shout at me, but then suddenly he smiled.

"Don't move," I said. "I'll get the **vacuum**."

———

The King's Head pub was busy that evening. I sat with Patrick and his friends from the running club, and I drank my **wine**. The others were drinking orange juice. "Phil ran fifteen miles today," one of them said. "He couldn't even walk at the end of it!"

It was very cold outside, but Patrick was wearing a T-shirt. His body was hard and strong. I could feel the other men looking at my body and thinking that I needed to train, too.

"It was awful," I said to Patrick. "His girlfriend and his best friend."

"But you can understand it," replied Patrick. "He's in a wheelchair. And you say he's horrible to you. Maybe he was horrible to her, too."

"I don't know . . ." I thought of the picture of them both together. "They looked like they were very happy before the accident."

But Patrick wasn't listening. "Hey, Jim," he said, "did you try that new bike? Any good?"

After a few minutes, he went to buy me another glass of wine. When he came back, he said, "What do you think about going on holiday?"

"A holiday where?" I replied.

"Spain?" he said, looking excited. "So I can do a **triathlon** in August – sixty miles on a bike, thirty miles of running and a long swim in the sea."

"I've just got a job that is only for six months. I shouldn't ask Will's mother for a holiday," I replied. But I was also thinking how strange my boyfriend was now. Before he became a **personal trainer**, Patrick worked in an office and ate lots of chocolate. I liked him better then.

"You can do the triathlon with me," he said, but we both knew that he did not believe it.

"No, you do it. I'll sit by the pool," I said, and then I ordered myself some cake.

CHAPTER FIVE
Will becomes ill

After that day, things slowly began to get better. Will started to laugh more – usually at *me* – and one afternoon he started to ask me questions about my life.

"Tell me about yourself," he said. "What do you do when you're not watching films, Louisa?"

"I don't know," I said. "I go for a drink at the pub. I watch telly. I watch my boyfriend running."

"You watch *him* running?" he said. "But what do *you* like to do? Where do you like to go?"

I tried to think. "I don't know. I read a bit. I like clothes. My family go on holiday to Wales sometimes."

"And what do you want from your life? Do you want to get married? Have children? Do you want to have a great job and travel the world?"

I was silent while I thought about this. I knew that he would not like my answer. "I don't know," I said, finally. "I've never really thought about it."

In March, Will suddenly became ill. It started on a day with heavy snow. Will's father opened the door to the annexe as I walked towards it. "He's in bed," he said. "He's not feeling good. His mother is in London today."

"Where's Nathan?" I asked.

"He's not working this morning." Then he moved past

me and started walking towards the house, and I knew that he was happy to leave Will with me. "You know what he needs," he called over his shoulder.

I made Will a drink and pushed open the door to his bedroom. "Yes?" a voice said, quietly.

"Will, are you OK?" I said. "Do you need some pills?"

"Yes," he replied. "Strong ones for the pain."

I went to the kitchen and got some pills and some water. "Thank you," he said, quietly, after he swallowed them, and this worried me. Will did not usually thank me.

He closed his eyes, and I stood and watched him. His body lifted and fell under his T-shirt, and his mouth was open.

The snow fell and fell. Nathan came at lunchtime and gave Will some **antibiotics**. "Will's body can't work like ours," he explained. "If he gets an **infection**, his body gets really hot, and it can't **cool** itself down. Can you find a wet towel? We need to cool him down."

Nathan took off Will's clothes and put a sheet over him. I was surprised to see long, red lines from cuts on Will's arms. But I did not say anything, and Nathan did not say anything either.

It took forty minutes for Will's body to cool. Then Nathan showed me how to change Will's bag when he needed the toilet and how to change the **dressing** on his **tube**. "Because you may have to do it later," he explained.

After Nathan left, I stayed in Will's room. I sat in a chair and read a book of short stories. It was warm and silent in the annexe, and outside the world was white and beautiful.

At 5 p.m., I got a text message from Mrs Traynor.

```
There   are   no   trains   because   of   the
snow, so I can't get home. Will's father is
also in London. Could you stay the night?
Nathan can't stay.
```

I did not have to think about it. No problem, I wrote back. Then I called my parents and Patrick to tell them.

Will slept while I cooked myself some dinner, and then I took in a drink to him. His body was still quite warm, but he looked much better. I lifted him across to the other side of the bed.

"Why aren't you at home?" he said.

"It's OK. I'm staying," I said. It was dark outside now. I sat next to him on the bed. He turned his face towards me.

"Talk to me, Clark. Where did the crazy-clothes thing come from?" he asked, tiredly.

I smiled down at my pink jeans. "I've always loved bright colours. When I was a child, I had a pair of black-and-yellow tights. I never took them off. Then Mum threw them away, and I cried for days."

"Why did she do that?" he asked.

"Because they were old and had lots of holes in them," I replied. "But I loved those tights more than anything."

We talked a bit more about my love of clothes, and then Will went to sleep. I changed the sheet on top of him to keep him cool and then sat back down next to him, and soon I slept, too.

Winter slowly changed into spring, and in April warmer weather came. One morning, I was **shaving** Will for the first time and was planning to cut his hair, when a young woman suddenly came running in and started shouting at him. Then Mrs Traynor came in behind her and cried, "Georgina, please don't shout!"

"How could you try to do it, Will?" the young woman cried. "Why did you do that?"

Then Mrs Traynor turned to me. "Please leave us and go for your lunch, Louisa."

I quickly went out and walked around the streets for half

an hour. I knew that Georgina was Will's sister, but she lived in Australia. Why was she back?

When I came back, the annexe door was open. I stopped and listened. "Isn't there anything that they can do?" Georgina was asking.

"Look," Mrs Traynor replied, "we didn't want to tell you, but Daddy found him in January. He tried to kill himself."

When I heard this, I thought of the red lines on his arms, and my body went cold.

"He promised me six months, Georgina," Mrs Traynor continued. "I have to try to **change his mind** before August. Or he will go to Switzerland, to **Dignitas** in Zurich."

"And the girl?" asked Georgina.

"Louisa is here to stop him from trying to kill himself again," replied Mrs Traynor.

CHAPTER SIX
Lou and Treena make a plan

I decided to leave my job at the end of the day. While Will was watching television with his father, I found a sheet of paper and wrote a letter to Mrs Traynor, which I left in her kitchen. Then I left without saying goodbye.

When I got home, Mrs Traynor's expensive car was already waiting outside my house. "Can we talk?" she said through the car window. "Please, just for five minutes."

So I got into the car.

"I thought you and Will were friends," she said. "What's the problem – is it the money?"

"I heard you and Georgina talking," I said. "And I don't want to be part of your plan."

She was silent for a moment. Then she said, "Please don't leave, Louisa. Will likes you. It will be hard to find another person now."

"But you're taking him to Dignitas."

"No," she said and shook her head. "I'm trying to *stop* him from going to Switzerland. I thought you were happy and funny. You weren't like a nurse. And you *do* make him happy, Louisa. He allowed you to *shave* him and cut his hair! Please come back – I'll double your money."

"I don't want your money!" I shouted. "Don't you see? It's all lies. You've lied to me."

She swallowed. "I know, and I'm sorry. But think about it over the weekend. Please come back, Louisa. Please come back and help him."

I went into the house and went straight to my bedroom. Five minutes later, Treena appeared at the door. "Was that Mrs Traynor outside?" she said. "What's happened?"

"I've left my job," I said. "And I know Mum and Dad won't be happy. But . . ." And then I told her about Will and Dignitas, because I *had* to tell someone.

Treena thought for a bit. Then she suddenly said, "Look, it's easy. The Traynors have a lot of money, don't they? So they have to help you to change Will's mind. At the moment, he's at home all the time, isn't he? So, of course he's unhappy. Well, you have to get him out. Take him to music **concerts**, or to watch football. Or to another country. Do things that will make him happy."

I looked at my sister, and she looked back at me, and we suddenly both laughed. "Treena . . ." I said.

"I know," she joked. "I'm very, very clever!"

Mr and Mrs Traynor looked surprised when I told them my idea on Monday. And Georgina looked angry. "You mean *you* want to go with him on these adventures," she said. "I'm sure that *you* will have a very good time."

"Yes, I will go with him," I said. "I don't know what's possible yet. But I want to get him out of the house. Maybe we'll start close to home, and then we can take longer journeys later."

"Well, I think it's a great idea," said Mr Traynor. "And if you're going back to Australia, Georgina . . ."

"My new job starts in two weeks," Georgina said, quickly. "I told you – this is just a visit. I have a life, too, you know."

"Let's talk about this another time," said Mrs Traynor, but she did not look happy with her daughter. Then she turned to me. "All right, Louisa. Let's do it. You tell me your plans, and then I'll see how much money you are going to need."

———————

"You look happy," said Will when I came in through the door a week later.

"That's because we're going horse racing," I replied.

"Horse racing?" he said, surprised.

"Yes, at Longfield. If we leave now, we can be there for the third race. I have money on *Man Oh Man*. When he wins, I'm buying us lunch."

Nathan laughed when he heard this. "Sounds like a great idea!" he said.

I wanted it to be a perfect day, but everything quickly went wrong. It started with the car park's wet grass. The chair would not move on it, so Nathan and I had to lift Will over the grass, and we all got dirty. Then it became colder and started to rain. We watched three races, but Will did not want to put any money on the horses. He just watched silently. Then *Man Oh Man* lost his race.

When I turned round, Will's eyes were closed.

"Are you OK, Will?" I said. "Do you need something?"

He lifted his eyes to mine and said nothing.

"Let's get some lunch," I said to Nathan.

But when we got to the restaurant, we did not have the right tickets. "This restaurant is for *Premier* tickets only," the woman said.

"Please, let us in," I said. "You have empty tables, and he needs to be warm."

"Louisa, I want to go home," Will said, suddenly.

"No!" I said, and I was nearly crying.

Nathan put his hand on my arm. "Lou, Will's not hungry, and he wants to go home."

We carried Will back across the wet grass, and I drove him home. He was silent as I followed him inside the annexe. After Nathan went home, I changed Will's wet shoes and trousers and lit the fire. Then I put on the television.

"What's wrong?" I said, finally.

He was quiet for a moment, and then he said, "I don't like horse racing, Clark. Why didn't you ask me if I like it?"

I swallowed. "I thought that . . ."

"But you *didn't think*. You did what everyone always does . . . You decided what I wanted to do, and you didn't ask me." Then he turned his chair away from me and went into his bedroom.

CHAPTER SEVEN
The concert

I felt terrible about the horse racing and was not sure what to do next, so I was surprised when, a few weeks later, Will told me about a friend of his who played the **violin**. "He's playing in a concert near Stortford next week," he said and passed me his friend's CD. "He's given me tickets. You should go."

"I've never been to a concert," I replied. "Well, I did go to see Robbie Williams, but that's not the same. I would feel strange going to a posh violin concert."

"Then you should go. It's always good to try new things," he said.

I looked at the CD cover. "I'll go if you come with me."

He sat there silently for a few moments. "God, you're difficult," he said, finally.

———————

I remembered the horse racing, and this time I called first and checked that the concert would be OK for a disabled person. "Yes, of course. You have the best tickets because you can sit at the front," a woman told me. "We can even come and meet you when you arrive, if it helps."

It took me many hours to decide what to wear. Finally, I chose a red dress that always made me feel good. Then I put a white scarf round my shoulders.

"Wow!" said Nathan when I entered the room.

39

Will looked up and down at the dress and smiled. He was wearing a suit, and, with his shaved face and newly cut hair, he suddenly looked very handsome.

"You look great, Clark," he said.

It took forty minutes for me and Will to drive to the concert. When we got there, I followed Will to the front. The people tried to be polite, but I knew that they were looking at Will, because people always looked at him.

We sat down, and soon the **violinists** came out and started to play. Suddenly, I felt the music going through my body. My skin felt strange, and my hands were a bit wet. It was the most beautiful sound in the world. I looked at Will. His eyes were closed, and he looked like he was somewhere far away.

While I was driving home, I kept hearing the violins in my head.

"So, you didn't enjoy it?" Will said. I looked into the mirror and saw that he was smiling at me.

I smiled back at him. "I loved it!" I said. "Thank you. Thank you for taking me."

I started to open the car door but suddenly he said, "Don't, Clark. I want to sit for a few minutes. I just want to be a man who has been to a concert with a girl in a red dress."

I took my hand from the door. "OK," I said.

I was at the running club. Patrick was jumping up and down in his new Nike T-shirt. "I'm sorry I can't come to the pub this evening," I said. "But I have to help with Will's pills and change his tube dressing because Nathan can't come."

"Well, you'll have to come next week." He lifted his foot, then pushed it against the ground. "We are going to talk about the triathlon. And you haven't told me what you want to do for your birthday next week."

"Mum's cooking a special meal," I said. "Treena went to college last week, so Mum's a bit sad. She invited Will."

I did not **expect** Will to come to my birthday meal, so I was very surprised when he said yes. My mother did not expect it either, and my parents went a bit crazy moving the furniture around and worrying about the wheelchair. Dad even made a ramp for the door.

I opened the front door at 7.30 p.m. to see Will sitting outside in his wheelchair with Nathan behind him. Will was wearing a suit.

Mum and Dad stood behind me as Will came into the sitting room. Then Nathan left us. "Hello, Will!" Dad said, touching Will's shoulder. "It's good to meet you finally! I'm Bernard, and this is Josie. I hope the ramp was OK. What will you drink?"

My mum smiled at him, and Will smiled back. "Pleased to meet you," he said. "I've got some very expensive French wine in my bag, Clark. You must have good wine on your birthday."

As I took the bottle of wine from the bag that was hanging from the back of Will's chair, Patrick suddenly appeared at the front door. "Hi, sorry I'm late," he said. "So you are Will. Here, I'll open that," said Patrick, taking the bottle of wine from me.

Then Will came to the dinner table, and we all sat down. Grandad was there, too. Everyone began to talk. Dad was telling Will funny stories about me, and Will was laughing.

But I noticed that Patrick was not saying much, and he kept looking at Will all the time while I was feeding him with a spoon. "Stop looking," I thought.

Later, everyone gave me presents. Patrick gave me a little blue ring. It was beautiful, but I did not like wearing rings.

"And I've got something for you in my bag," said Will.

I went to his bag and found a small bag. Inside it were some yellow-and-black tights. "Oh, these are wonderful!" I said. "Where did you get them?"

"A lady made them for me," said Will.

"Tights?" said Dad and Patrick together.

"They are the best tights in the world!" I replied.

"They're the same as the ones you wore when you were small," said Mum, and Will and I both smiled.

Will stayed for another hour, and then Nathan came back to get him. "You're a lucky man," Will said to Patrick when he was leaving. "She gives great bed baths."

"You didn't tell me that you give him bed baths," Patrick said later in the evening, when Will was not there and my parents were in the kitchen.

"I don't," I replied. "He's joking with you, Patrick! Are you jealous of him?"

"I'm *not* jealous of him," said Patrick. "How can I be jealous of someone who is disabled?"

CHAPTER EIGHT
A wedding invitation

May was a strange month. The newspapers were full of stories about people who wanted to die at Dignitas. A famous footballer was hurt in an accident, and he killed himself because he could not go to Dignitas. Another woman, who was very ill, wanted her husband to take her there. But she did not want him to go to prison for it. I knew that Will was reading these stories on his computer, too, which he used with **voice-recognition software**.

Will and I were going out a lot now. We went to the theatre, and to more concerts, and to the cinema. And sometimes, when the weather was good, we went out in Stortford. I just walked around with him, beside his wheelchair. Then, suddenly, Dad was made redundant at the furniture factory. He tried to be brave about it and went straight to the job centre. "I will **apply** for anything," he said. But it was going to be hard for a fifty-five-year-old man to find a job.

On the Friday after Dad stopped working, Will got an invitation to Lissa and Rupert's wedding. "Do you want to keep it?" I said, looking at the expensive invitation with its gold writing.

"I don't care," Will said. "Do what you want with it."

———

"What's the best place you've ever visited?" I asked Will one windy afternoon in May. We were sitting in front of the castle and watching the tourists walk by.

"I climbed Mount Kilimanjaro when I was thirty," he said. "That was beautiful. Oh, and I loved Mauritius. Lovely people and beautiful beaches. What about you?"

"I've not really been anywhere very interesting," I said. "What do you think? Where should I go?"

"I don't know, but you have to go somewhere. You're too interesting to stay here all your life. Maybe you should go to college and study fashion." He thought for a moment. Then he smiled and said, "There's a wonderful café in a part of Paris called Le Marais. I liked sitting outside it and eating warm bread with butter and jam. That's where you should go."

I turned to look at him. "We *could* go," I said. "I've never been to Paris. I'd love to go."

"No," he said. "I don't want to go there in this wheelchair. I want to be the *old* me, with pretty French girls looking at me when they walk past. I don't want them to see me in this wheelchair."

"OK," I said, and then I was quiet. I was becoming very worried that he wasn't going to change his mind about Dignitas. I knew that Mrs Traynor was worried, too, because she came to see me the next day. We talked a bit about my family and how difficult it was to share a room with my sister, who was coming home from college soon. "You can always stay in the other room here," she said.

45

Then she said, "How are things?"

"Well, we're going out a lot more," I said. "And he talks a lot more than he did."

She nodded. "He talks to *you* but not me," she said. "Have you talked about going to another country with him? My husband and I have been talking about it, and we both think it's a good idea."

We were both silent for a few moments. Then she said, "We only have two and a half months until August."

"I'm doing everything that I can, Mrs Traynor," I replied.

She nodded. "I know, Louisa."

CHAPTER NINE
A lawyer visits Will

June came, and little changed. Will and I continued to go out to places, and he was happier, but he never spoke about Dignitas. I tried to think of more things to do. But there are so many things you *cannot* do with a quadriplegic person. I made a list of them.

Things Will cannot do
1. Go on a train in London
2. Go swimming without help, or in a cold pool
3. Go on a beach
4. Go shopping in shops without ramps
5. Go anywhere quickly, because we have to plan
6. Go to restaurants without ramps (and he does not like people seeing me give him food)
7. Go to friends' houses that don't have ramps
8. Go where there are crowds of people

One afternoon, I came home to find Dad at the front door. He was smiling at me. "There you are," he said. "You'll have to make yourself tea tonight. I'm taking your mother out for dinner."

"Oh no. Did I miss her birthday?" I asked, quickly.

"No," he said, and he put his arms around me. He was laughing, and he suddenly looked much younger. "Guess what happened today, Lou? I got a job!"

"Dad, that's wonderful!" I shouted. "What's the job?"

"I'm going to be looking after the furniture in the castle."

I was quiet for a second. Then I said, "But that's Will's father's . . ."

"Mr Traynor called me," Dad continued. "Will told him about me, so he knew that I was looking for a job."

"You're working for Will's dad?" I said.

Then Mum came up behind Dad. She was wearing her best dress and shoes, and she looked really happy. "It's good money, Lou," she said. "More than the furniture factory!"

"That's . . . that's great, Dad, really . . ." I said, finally. And I put my arms around them both.

"You should thank Will," Dad said. "What a lovely man! Please, thank him for thinking of me."

As soon as they left, I called Will. It took him a few minutes to answer. I thought of him driving himself to the hands-free phone.

"Hello?"

"Did you do this?" I asked. "Did you get Dad this job?"

"Yes. Aren't you pleased?" he said.

"I am pleased," I replied. "But it feels strange."

"Well, don't feel strange," he said. "Your dad needed a job. My dad needed a man who knows about furniture. And it means that you can do what you want to do now. Your parents don't need your money from this job any more. You can go travelling, or to college."

I felt like his words were hitting me. His words really meant that soon he would not need me any more. He was *still planning to die.*

"Lou? You're being very quiet," he said.

"I'm sorry. I've got to go," I said, quickly. And I put down the phone.

I went to the pub to find Patrick. The air was filled with the smell of flowers, and the tourists smiled when they passed me on the street.

"Can I get you a drink?" Patrick asked when I entered the pub. He was with his friends from the running club.

"In a minute," I replied. Then I told Patrick about Dad's job. He did not look happy.

"So now you're *both* working for Will Traynor?" he said.

I wanted to tell him then about Will. I wanted him to know that I was trying to save Will's life. But I knew that Will's plans were a secret.

"And I may stay there for a bit, too," I said. "In the other bedroom. Treena is coming back from college soon for the summer holidays, and I don't want to share a room again."

"Why don't you come and live with me?" Patrick said. "We've been together for seven years. It's time you moved in with me, isn't it?"

"Really? You really want to live together?" I said, surprised.

"Yes, I'm sure. It will be good," he said, but he did not look happy.

The next evening, I moved into Patrick's flat.

When I was at the annexe the next day, a man came to the door. He was wearing an expensive suit.

"Hi, I'm Michael Lawler, Will's lawyer," he said. "I'm here to see Will."

"Let him in," said Will, appearing behind me. "We'll be in the sitting room, Louisa. Please can you make us some coffee and then leave us?"

"Um, OK . . ." I said.

Mr Lawler stayed for about an hour. When he finally appeared again, Will was behind him. "Thank you, Michael," Will said. He did not look at me. "I'll wait to hear from you."

That evening, I looked for *Michael Lawler, lawyer*, on the internet. The third name that appeared read: *Michael Lawler, Lawyer for **wills and probate***. Will was getting ready to die!

I was **horrified**. I waited a few days, and then I rang Mrs Traynor and asked her to meet me away from the house. We met at a small café in town. I immediately told her about Michael Lawler's visit.

She looked horrified, too. "A *wills and probate* lawyer? Are you sure?" she said.

I nodded. "I checked him on the internet."

She was quiet for a moment. Then she said, "Have you

thought of any other ideas for things to do with Will? What about that holiday?"

I told her about Paris and my list of things that disabled people cannot do.

"Take him anywhere," she said, finally. "I'll pay for it."

When I got back, Will was waiting for me.

"What are you doing on Saturday?" he asked.

"Um, nothing," I replied. "Patrick's away training all day. Why?"

He smiled. "We're going to a wedding."

CHAPTER TEN
The wedding

I never knew why Will changed his mind about Lissa and Rupert's wedding. Maybe he wanted to be difficult. Or maybe he just wanted everything finished in his mind.

We decided that we did not need Nathan to come with us. I called to check that the **marquee** was OK for a wheelchair, and Lissa promised to get us a ramp. She sounded surprised and worried.

I decided to wear the red dress that Will liked. I did not have any other dresses that were right for a posh wedding anyway.

I did not tell Will, but I was worried. I did not know why he wanted to go and see his ex-girlfriend marry his best friend – did he really want to hurt himself even more?

The morning of the wedding was bright and sunny. Nathan came early to get Will ready for us to leave at 9 a.m. It was a two-hour drive to Lissa's parents' house, which was large and old, with white flowers around its tall windows. I took Will straight to the church. He was smiling and looked happy.

"Relax, Clark," he said. "It's going to be fine."

I put out the ramp and helped him out of the car. "So, how are you going to be today?" I asked. "Angry? Or are you planning something terrible?"

Will looked at me, but his eyes did not show his feelings. "We're going to be very good, Louisa," he said, and then he smiled again.

The wedding went well. Lissa looked very beautiful in her long white dress. The women watching all had fashionable shoes and huge hats, and the men wore expensive suits.

Will and I sat at the back of the church. He looked up quickly when Lissa walked past, but I did not know what he was feeling. Then suddenly the wedding was finished, and Will was driving himself out of the church.

"Are you OK?" I called, running behind him.

"I'm fine," he said. "Come on, let's get a drink."

The marquee was in the garden. The bar was at the back, and there were already lots of people around it. The waiters were only giving us a strange pink drink called Pimms. "Other drinks will be served later," they told me.

"Two, please," I said. Then I looked down at the pink drink. "They have all that money, but they don't want to pay for **alcohol**," I thought.

When I got back to Will, he was talking to lots of people. Many of them knew him and were happy to see him. Lissa walked around the garden kissing people and talking to them, but she did not come to us.

Lunch was soup followed by fish. I sat next to Will and fed him. Everyone was drinking wine and beer now, but I continued drinking Pimms because I was driving. But I was beginning to feel quite strange.

"Is there any alcohol in Pimms?" I asked Will.

"Each one has about the same amount of alcohol as in a glass of wine," he replied.

I looked at him, horrified. "You're joking? I thought it had no alcohol in it. How am I going to drive you home?"

He laughed. "It's all right, Clark. There's a good hotel up the road. Ring them and see if we can stay there. I'll pay for it."

I looked for the number of the hotel on my phone. Then I called them.

"So?" he said, when I finished the call.

"Yes, the hotel has got rooms, and there's no problem about the wheelchair," I replied. "So we can stay there."

"That's good," he said. "Now please drink. It will make me very happy to see you get drunk when Lissa's father is paying for the drinks."

So I did. And the evening was lovely. The lights were turned down, and I could smell flowers on the evening air. There was music and dancing, and suddenly everyone on our table was relaxed and laughing.

"Don't you want to dance, Louisa?" asked a nice woman called Mary, who was sitting on the other side of Will. She knew him well, and it was good to see them talking and laughing together.

"Please, no!" I replied.

A little later, Lissa came to our table. "Thank you for coming, Will," she said, and she kissed him on the cheek. Then she looked quickly at me.

"Thank you for the invitation," Will replied. "You look lovely, Lissa. It's been a great day."

And then at 10 p.m. the slow dances started. We watched Lissa and Rupert move around the dance floor. When the dance finished, more people joined them.

I turned to Will. "Would you like to dance?" I said. "Come on, let's give these people something to talk about." Then I sat carefully across Will's knees and lifted my arms around his neck. He looked into my eyes for a moment, then drove himself on to the dance floor and started moving in small circles. I closed my eyes and

put my face against his. I could hear him singing to the music.

I opened my eyes for a moment and saw Lissa watching us over Will's shoulder. Her face was angry and unhappy. As soon as she saw me watching her, she turned away and said something to Rupert, who shook his head.

"Do you know something, Clark?" Will said.

I lifted my head and looked into his eyes.

"Sometimes you are the only thing that makes me want to wake up in the morning."

"Then let's go somewhere," I said, quickly, before I could think about it.

"What?"

"Let's have a week together somewhere where we can have fun," I continued. "Just you and me. Please say yes."

His eyes did not leave mine. "OK," he said, finally.

CHAPTER ELEVEN
A perfect holiday

Patrick and I were on the hills outside town when I told him about the holiday. He was doing a sixteen-mile run, and I was following him on my bicycle.

"You what?" he shouted over his shoulder.

"I'm not coming to the triathlon in Spain," I said. "I'm going away with Will. I'm . . . I'm working."

Patrick turned to look at me with his legs still moving under him. "But I thought that you were coming to watch me? Why can't they get a nurse to go with him?" And he began to run faster. I could see that he was very angry, and I knew that I had to tell him.

"Patrick!" I shouted. "He wants to die, Patrick! He wants to kill himself."

Patrick immediately slowed. "Say that again?"

And so I told him. I told him about Dignitas and Will's promise to his mother. "I know that it sounds crazy," I said, "but I have to change his mind. I'm sorry, I wanted to tell you before, but I couldn't."

He did not answer, and he still looked angry. He swallowed twice, and then he said, "Lou, we have been together for seven years, and you've known this man for five months. If you go with him now, you are telling me something about how you feel about us. Don't you understand?"

"That's not true. I . . ."

"I want to run by myself now, Louisa, OK?" he said, and he turned away.

I was silent for a moment, and then I said, "OK. I think it's best if we finish things. I won't stay with you tonight."

———

That evening, Nathan called me. "Will is ill again," he said. "This is his third infection in two years – and his worst because now he's in hospital."

I immediately went to the hospital and found Will lying in bed with tubes coming out of him. He had a mask over his mouth and nose, and his eyes were closed. Mrs Traynor sat next to him.

"He's a bit better," she said, tiredly. "They are giving him strong antibiotics. Will you stay with him while I go home and get some clothes?"

"Of course."

The days and nights went past. I heard nothing from Patrick, but it did not matter. I sat and held Will's hand and looked into his face. On day three, when he slowly opened his eyes, I stood over him and lifted his mask. "How are you feeling?" I asked, trying not to cry.

"I've been better," he replied.

While I was sitting with Will, I used my phone to look for holidays for disabled people. I needed to find somewhere where he could relax and get better. Finally, I found a holiday that was perfect.

———

Ten days later, Mr Traynor drove us to Gatwick Airport, and we flew to Mauritius. Nathan came with us. The twelve-hour flight went well, but Will was quiet and did not eat very much. When we arrived, a driver took us to the hotel. The island was beautiful and green, and the sea around us was a deep blue.

Will slept for the first two days. But then, suddenly, he started to look better. His face had colour in it, and he began to eat again, in the hotel's three restaurants.

I began to enjoy myself, too, and I slowly saw that this was the most beautiful place in the world. Our days had a nice routine. Every day, we took Will to the tables around the swimming pool for breakfast. Then we went to the beach. It wasn't as difficult on the beach with Will's wheelchair as I thought it would be. I read, and Will sat with his eyes closed listening to music. Nathan usually swam. Sometimes, we helped Will into the warm water and he looked happy and relaxed. His skin became brown, and he stopped wearing a shirt.

For lunch, we went to one of the restaurants, and then we spent the hot afternoons in our rooms before meeting again in the evening. Then we all ate and drank wine and talked about our lives.

On the fourth night, Nathan met a girl, and they went out to a restaurant. Will and I were alone. That night, I sat on the bed next to him. There was a big storm, and we watched the wind and rain through the window with our legs touching. Then I held his hand. He turned his head and smiled at me.

"Not bad, is it, Clark?" he said.

"No," I said. "Not bad at all."

On the last night, Will and I went to the beach together. Nathan was out with his girlfriend. I was wearing a white dress, and I had a flower in my hair. The night was warm, and I could smell the sea. We sat under our favourite tree.

"Are you glad that you came?" I asked.

He nodded. "Oh, yes. You are wonderful, Clark."

I looked at him, and then I moved forward and kissed him, and he kissed me back. And just for a moment, I could smell his skin and feel his soft hair under my fingers, and it was just Will and me on this beautiful island, with the night sky above us.

Then, suddenly, he pulled back. "I can't," he said.

"Why? I don't understand," I replied.

He swallowed. "Because I can't be the man I want to be with you."

I continued to hold his face in my hands. "Listen, Will, I know about Dignitas. I don't care what you can and can't do. I know this isn't a normal love story. But *I love you*, Will. I knew it when I left Patrick. And I think you love me, too."

For a moment, he just looked at me. Then he said, very quietly, "I'm sorry. It's not enough."

"I don't understand."

"I know that this could be a good life," he went on.

"Maybe *very* good with you around. But it's not *my* life. I loved my life before the accident, Clark. I liked riding my motorbike. I liked climbing mountains and bungee jumping. I don't want to live in this wheelchair. I'm going to get more and more ill. You saw what I was like in the hospital when I had that infection."

I was crying now. "Please, Will, don't say this. Please try."

"No," he said. "I'm going to Dignitas on 13th August, and if you *really* love me, you will come with me."

I stood up then. "No," I said. "I tell you that I love you, but you want me to come and watch you kill yourself?"

"Louisa . . ."

"Don't!" I shouted. "Don't say another word. How can you ask me to do that? Why did I take this stupid job?"

And then I ran up the beach and back to my hotel room.

CHAPTER TWELVE
A normal house

We flew home without speaking, and I left Will with Mr and Mrs Traynor as soon as we got to Stortford. They gave me some strange looks, but I did not want to speak to them about it. I went straight home to my parents and stayed in my room for three days. After that, I only spoke to Treena, and I did not go out.

Then, on 12th August, Mrs Traynor called me.

———

Treena drove me straight to the airport.

"I've changed my mind, and I have to go," I told her. "I've *changed* because of him, Treena. It's because of him that I have started to think about going to college. I love him, and he has to decide what's best for him. But I don't want him to be alone when he dies."

I flew into Zurich Airport at midnight and went straight to a hotel. The next morning, a taxi took me to Dignitas. I did not know what to expect from the building, but it looked like a normal house, with factories and a football field next to it.

A woman opened the door and knew who I was. "He is here," she said. "Shall I take you to him?"

I stood still for a moment, feeling frightened. Then I breathed **deeply** and nodded.

I saw the bed before I saw him. It was huge and white.

Mrs Traynor sat on one side, and Mr Traynor sat on the other. Georgina was in a chair in the corner, and her eyes were red from crying.

Will looked at me and smiled, and I smiled back. "Nice room," I joked.

Then Will turned to his mother. "I want to talk to Lou. Is that OK?"

She tried to smile, but I knew that she was thinking many things at the same time. "Of course," she said. Then she, Mr Traynor and Georgina left the room, and it was just us.

"I'm not going to try and change your mind," I said. Then, "I missed you."

He relaxed then. "Come over here," he said. "Sit on the bed. Next to me."

I lay down and put my arm across him. Then I lifted my head and laid it on his shoulder. I could feel his fingers on my back and his soft breathing in my hair. I said nothing, but tried to feel him and remember him, this man who I loved.

Then I heard his voice say quietly in my ear, "Hey, Clark, tell me something good."

So I told him a story of two people who did not like each other much when they first met. But later, they learned that they were the only two people who really understood each other. I told him about their adventures and journeys, and the help that they gave each other. And while I spoke, I knew how important these words were to him. I told him something good.

Time slowed. It was just the two of us, with me talking, in the empty, sunny room. Will did not say much. Sometimes he nodded or made a small sound.

"It has been," I finished, "the best six months of my life."

There was a long silence. Then he said, "Funnily enough, Clark, mine too."

And then I began to cry. I held him and cried and cried.

"Don't, Clark," he said. I felt him kiss my head. "Look at me."

I shook my head.

"Look at me, please."

I lifted my head. His eyes looked clear and relaxed.

"You look so beautiful," he said. And then he kissed

me, and we held each other and we said nothing, but my body told him that he was loved.

We stayed like that for a long time, and then finally I felt him breathe deeply, and he pulled his head back so that we could see each other.

"Clark," he said, quietly. "Can you call my parents in?"

———————

I sat in front of the dark green café, looking down the Rue des Francs Bourgeois. It was a beautiful, sunny autumn day in Paris. Then I drank some of my coffee and smiled at the plate of warm bread, butter and jam in front of me. I put my hand over my eyes in front of the sun and watched a woman play with her hair in front of a shop window.

Then I breathed deeply, before taking the letter out of my bag.

Only to be read in the Café Marquis, Rue des Francs Bourgeois, Paris, with warm bread and jam.

The letter was written using the voice-recognition software on Will's computer.

Clark,
It will be autumn now. I hope the coffee is good and the bread is warm, and that it is still sunny enough to sit outside. There are a few things that I want to say.

When you get back to England, take this letter to Michael Lawler. He has money for you. It is enough to pay for the college course you talked about and living costs while you are studying. It will also buy you somewhere nice to live.

I am not giving this money to you to say thank you. I'm giving it to you because there is not much that makes me happy any more, but you do. I want to know that I have helped you to live a good life, a better life. Knowing this helps me. You are braver than you think you are, Clark. I can see it. So please live well, wear those black-and-yellow tights and be happy.

You have touched my heart. You did it the first day you arrived, with your crazy clothes and your bad jokes.

You changed my life much more than this money will ever change yours.

Don't be sad. Just live well.

Love, Will

During-reading questions

Write the answers to these questions in your notebook.

CHAPTER ONE

1 What kind of holiday does Lissa want? What kind of holiday does Will want?
2 What do we learn about Will in this chapter?
3 Why does Will get hit by the car?

CHAPTER TWO

1 What does Lou like about her job at the Buttered Bun Café?
2 Why does she lose her job there?
3 Why is Lou's dad angry when she loses the job?

CHAPTER THREE

1 What goes well in Lou's interview with Camilla Traynor? What goes badly, do you think?
2 What does Will do when he first meets Lou? Why does he do this, do you think?
3 Who is Nathan, and how does he feel about Will?

CHAPTER FOUR

1 What things does Lou see in Will's bedroom? What do these things show her about him?
2 Is Will nice to Lou when he first meets her? Give reasons for your answer.
3 Why do Lissa and Rupert visit Will?
4 How does Will feel about their visit?

CHAPTER FIVE

1 The chapter begins: "After that day, things slowly began to get better." How do they get better?
2 Why does Nathan give Will antibiotics?
3 What does Lou learn about her job, and about Will?

CHAPTER SIX

1 Why does Lou leave her job?
2 What is Treena's idea?
3 What goes wrong at the horse racing?

CHAPTER SEVEN

1 How is Will and Lou's time at the concert better than at the horse racing?
2 How does Lou feel about the concert?
3 What is special about Will's birthday present to Lou?

CHAPTER EIGHT

1 What happens to Lou's dad?
2 What does Will get from Lissa? How does he feel about it?
3 Where does Will think that Lou should go?

CHAPTER NINE

1 How does Lou's dad get a job?
2 Why isn't Patrick happy when Lou tells him about her dad?
3 What does Michael Lawler's visit mean?

CHAPTER TEN

1 Why is Lou worried about Lissa's wedding?
2 Why does Lou choose to drink Pimms? Why is this a mistake?
3 How does Lissa feel about Will and Lou's dance, do you think?

CHAPTER ELEVEN

1 Why is Patrick angry about Lou's holiday with Will, do you think?
2 Where do Lou, Nathan and Will travel to? What is it like?
3 What do Will and Lou do on their last night together?
4 What does Will decide and what does Lou do?

CHAPTER TWELVE

1 Why does Lou change her mind about going to Dignitas, do you think?
2 What are the "good" things that Lou tells Will?
3 Where does Lou go at the end of the story?
4 What does Will give her?

After-reading questions

1 How did Lou change during the story? How did Will change?
2 Why did Will send Lou to Paris and give her his money, do you think?
3 How will the money change Lou's life, do you think?
4 What do you think the title *Me Before You* means?

Exercises

CHAPTER ONE

1 **Write the correct question words in your notebook.**

1 .....*Who*.... came out of the bathroom?

2 .... fell over Lissa's shoulder?

3 .... did Lissa want to go on holiday?

4 .... fell on to the road?

CHAPTER TWO

2 **Complete these sentences in your notebook, using the names from the box.**

Frank	Patrick	Lou's dad	Lou's mum	Syed

1 ....*Frank*........... owns a café but wants to go back to Australia.

2 .... is very angry because Lou only got three months' money.

3 .... thinks that Lou is clever and can train to do office work.

4 .... has a personal training business.

5 .... works at the job centre.

CHAPTER THREE

3 **Write the correct verbs in your notebook.**

1 Lou had to **wore** / *wear* a suit at the interview.

2 Camilla Traynor **wear** / **was wearing** an expensive-looking suit.

3 Lou heard the sound of her skirt **tore** / **tearing**.

4 She was frightened to **stand** / **standing** up.

5 For a moment, Lou could not **spoke** / **speak**.

6 Nathan **needs** / **need** to stay sometimes.

7 Lou must **vacuum** / **vacuuming** the floors.

73

4 **Who says these words? Who do they say them to?**
Write the correct names in your notebook.

1 "Ah, the girl who makes tea." ....*Will says this to Lou.*.........
2 "He hates me."
3 "We have to spend a lot of time together. Could you tell me more about yourself?"
4 "Everything all right?"
5 "So why have you come to see me? It's been eight months . . ."
6 "Actually, Rupert and I came because we have some news. We're getting married."
7 "We're only telling you because we care about you."
8 "You can do the triathlon with me."

CHAPTER FIVE

5 **In your notebook, match the words with the definitions.**
Example: 1 – c

1	annexe	**a**	a long, thin thing that liquid can move through
2	antibiotics	**b**	a problem in your body that comes from bacteria
3	infection	**c**	a small building that is next to a larger building
4	dressing	**d**	to change what you decided before
5	tube	**e**	something you put over a cut on your body
6	change your mind	**f**	an organization in Zurich, Switzerland, that helps very ill people to end their lives
7	Dignitas	**g**	a medicine that kills infections

CHAPTER SIX

6 **In your notebook, make these sentences negative.**

1 I decided to leave my job at the end of the day.
I decided not to leave my job at the end of the day.

2 "And you *do* make him happy, Louisa."

3 "You've lied to me."

4 Mr and Mrs Traynor looked surprised when I told them my idea.

5 We had the right tickets for the restaurant.

CHAPTER EIGHT

7 **Write questions for these answers in your notebook.**

1 *How was Will reading the newspaper stories?*
He was reading them on his computer with voice-recognition software.

2 He went straight to the job centre.

3 They were sitting in front of the castle.

4 He climbed Mount Kilimanjaro when he was thirty.

5 He thought that she should go to Le Marais in Paris.

CHAPTER NINE

8 **Correct these sentences in your notebook**

1 A lot changed in June.
Little changed in June.

2 Lou's dad was not happy about his new job.

3 Will's mother gave Lou's dad the job.

4 Patrick looked happy when Lou told him about her dad's job.

5 A doctor came to see Will.

6 Lou moved into Will's flat.

CHAPTER ELEVEN

9 **Are these sentences *true* or *false*?**

1 Lou was going away with Will because she did not want to go away with Patrick. ....*false*..........

2 Lou was going away with Will to try and change his mind about killing himself.

3 Lou wanted to finish her relationship with Patrick.

4 The flight to Mauritius took twenty-four hours.

5 Nathan met a girl on the holiday.

6 Will did not want to kiss Lou because he did not like her.

7 Will thought that he would get more and more ill.

8 Lou wanted to go to Dignitas with Will.

CHAPTER TWELVE

10 **Order the sentences by writing *1–8* in your notebook.**

a .... Will wanted his parents to come back into the room.

b .... Lou reads in Will's letter that he has given her a lot of money.

c .... Lou flew to Switzerland and stayed in a hotel before going to Dignitas.

d .... Will was waiting for her in a huge bed.

e .... Lou told Will good things about their time together.

f .... Lou changed her mind about going to Switzerland.

g ....*1*.... Lou and Will flew home without speaking.

h .... Lou went to Paris.

An answer key for all questions and exercises can be found at
www.penguinreaders.co.uk

11 **What happens here? Match the two parts of the sentences in your notebook.**

Example: 1 – c

1	The Buttered Bun	a	Lou read a letter from Will.
2	The annexe	b	Lou and Will started to kiss.
3	The horse races	c	Lou lost her job.
4	The concert	d	Will gave Lou some tights.
5	Lou's birthday	e	Will and Lou danced together.
6	Lissa's wedding	f	Lou listened to violins.
7	Mauritius	g	Lou lost a bet.
8	Paris	h	Will was ill, and Lou stayed with him.

Project work

1 You are Lou. Write a diary of your time with Will in Mauritius.

2 Write about the lives of disabled people in your country. How does your country help disabled people? Is there more that your country can do? Give ideas.

3 Write a newspaper report about Will's accident.

4 What happens to Lou after the story, do you think? Give reasons for your answers. Then look at information online about Jojo Moyes' two other stories about Lou, *After You* and *Still Me*, and see if you were right.

5 Compare the book to the film of *Me Before You*. How are they the same/different? Why did the writer make the changes for the film, do you think?

Glossary

alcohol (n.)
Alcohol is something in drinks like beer or *wine*. When people drink a lot of it, they become *drunk*.

antibiotics (n.)
medicines that kill *infections*

apply (v.)
If you *apply* for something, you write to ask if you can do or have it. People *apply* for jobs.

breathe (v.)
to take air into and out of your body through your nose and mouth

bungee jumping (n.)
the sport of jumping from a very high place with a long rope (= something long, thick and strong) on you. The rope pulls you back up before you hit the ground.

care assistant (n.)
someone who looks after old, *disabled* or very ill people

change your mind (phr.)
to change what you decided before

cheek (n.)
one of the two round parts of your face under your eyes

company (n.)
having other people with you

concert (n.)
when people play music or sing in a place and a lot of other people listen to them

cool (v.)
to become colder, or to make something become colder

deeply (adv.)
If you *breathe deeply*, you take a lot of air deep into your body through your nose and mouth.

Dignitas (pr. n.)
an organization (= a group of people who work together to do something) in Zurich, Switzerland, that helps very ill people to end their lives

disabled (adj. and v.)
If someone is *disabled*, they have a problem with their body or mind that makes it difficult for them to do the things that other people can do. If something *disables* someone, it makes them *disabled*.

dressing (n.)
something you put over a cut on your body. A *dressing* helps the cut to stay clean and stops *infections*.

drunk (adj.)
when you feel different because you have drunk *alcohol*. If you are *drunk*, sometimes you are not able to speak or do things in the way that you usually do them.

expect (v.)
to think that something will happen

feed (v.)
to give food to a person

finally (adv.)
after a long time

furniture (n.)
things in a room or building, like chairs, tables or beds

horrified (adj.)
very surprised and sad, or frightened

infection (n.)
a problem in your body that comes from bacteria (= very small living things that sometimes make you ill)

interview (n.)
when someone asks you lots of questions to decide if you will get a job

job centre (n.)
a special office where people who are looking for work can get information about jobs

joke (v.)
to say funny things

lift (v.)
to move someone or something up

magazine (n.)
a thin book with large pages and pictures. You can buy a new *magazine* every week or month.

marquee (n.)
a large tent (= house made of material) that is used for parties and shows

personal training (n.); **personal trainer** (n.)
A *personal trainer*'s job is to help someone to get a better body by showing them how to exercise (= do things like running and swimming). *Personal training* is when a *personal trainer* does this for someone.

pill (n.)
a very small, hard piece of medicine that you *swallow*

posh (adj.)
expensive and fashionable

quadriplegic (n. and adj.)
a person who is not able to move their arms, legs or other parts of their body. Some *quadriplegic* people can use their hands to move around in a *wheelchair*.

redundant (adj.)
If someone is made *redundant*, they are told to leave their job because there is not enough work.

reference (n.)
a letter about you that is written by someone who knows you. It is sent to someone who may give you a job.

relaxing (adj.); **relax** (v.)
when you do something relaxing, you feel happy and comfortable because you are not worried about anything

routine (n.)
the things that you usually do each day or week, and how or when you do them

shave (n. and v.)
to cut hair from a person's face or body. A *shave* is when someone does this to themselves or another person.

sheet (n.)
a big, thin piece of material for a bed. You lie on or under it.

shoulder (n.)
where your arm meets your body

silence (n.)
when no one speaks or makes a noise

suit (n.)
a jacket and trousers or skirt that are made from the same thing. You wear them together.

swallow (v.)
to make food or drink go from your mouth into your stomach. Sometimes you *swallow* before you speak because you are worried.

tear (v. and n.)
to make a hole in something by accident. A *tear* is the hole that you make.

tights (n.)
Women wear *tights* under their other clothes. They go over their legs, feet and bottom.

triathlon (n.)
a race where people must swim, ride a bicycle and run

tube (n.)
a long thin thing that liquid (= a thing like water) can move through

vacuum (v. and n.)
to clean something using a *vacuum* cleaner (= a machine that picks up dirt)

violin (n.); **violinist** (n.)
You play music on a *violin*. You put it against your neck and touch it with a long, thin piece of wood to make a sound. A *violinist* is someone who plays the *violin*.

voice-recognition software (n.)
a computer program that makes a computer understand a person's voice

wheelchair (n.)
a chair on wheels. People who are not able to walk use a *wheelchair* to move around.

wills and probate (n.)
A *will* is something that says who will get your money and other things you own when you die. *Probate* is when you show that a *will* is correct and allowed by law.

wine (n.)
a red or white drink made from grapes. *Wine* has *alcohol* in it.